THIS WALKER BOOK BELONGS TO:

_____

_____

_____

For Audrey and David

First published 2003 by Walker Books Ltd
87 Vauxhall Walk, London SE11 5HJ

This edition published 2004

4 6 8 10 9 7 5 3

© 2003 Penny Dale

This book has been typeset in GoudyHundred

Printed in China

British Library Cataloguing in Publication Data:
a catalogue record for this book is available from the British Library

ISBN-13: 978-1-84428-465-8
ISBN-10: 1-84428-465-4

www.walkerbooks.co.uk

Princess, Princess

Penny Dale

WALKER BOOKS
AND SUBSIDIARIES
LONDON • BOSTON • SYDNEY • AUCKLAND

There's a princess in a castle, sleeping, sleeping,
surrounded by her best friends, sleeping, sleeping.

For the longest time they've all been sleeping, sleeping.
Who will wake the princess with a kiss?

Once the princess spent her days
playing, playing,
dancing through the castle,
running, singing.

Riding on her horse,
playing in the garden,
playing with her best friends,
hiding, chasing.

Until one day the princess asked the fairies
to a party in the castle, her birthday party.

So they all came flitting, flying, bringing presents,
and everyone was happy to be there.

Except this frowning little fairy
whom the princess forgot to ask,
but still she came.
And when she saw the princess
playing without her,
what she wanted was to spoil the fun,
to spoil the game.

"Sleep, princess, sleep! Now all your games are over!"
The little fairy cast a spell.

"Sleep, sleep, with all your friends around you!
Sleep, sleep, until you're woken with a kiss!"

So the princess in the castle fell to sleeping,
surrounded by her best friends, sleeping, sleeping.

For the longest time they've all been sleeping, sleeping.
Who will wake the princess with a kiss?

For the longest time a forest has been growing around the castle, full of dreams, full of shadows.

There are no ways, no paths towards the castle.
Who will wake the princess with a kiss?

Who is flitting, flying through the shadows?
Who is flitting, flying through the trees?

Who is flitting, flying through the forest?

Who will wake the princess with a kiss?

The little fairy, sorry for her anger,
comes back at last
to break the sleeping spell.
Not frowning now,
but smiling, gently smiling...

The little fairy wakes

the princess with a kiss.

There's a princess in a castle, playing, playing, running, dancing, singing with her friends.

Skipping through the garden with a little fairy,
happy princess, happy fairy, happy friends.

WALKER BOOKS is the world's leading
independent publisher of children's books.
Working with the best authors and illustrators
we create books for all ages, from babies
to teenagers – books your child will
grow up with and always remember. So…

FOR THE BEST CHILDREN'S BOOKS,
LOOK FOR THE BEAR